A JOURNEY

OF FAITH

Dedication

I dedicate this book to my grandmother Ora Lee Beattie, my Aunt Carolyn Rooks, my cousin Du'juan Dowdy, and my best friend Tionne Wooten. For the love that we share together, and also because you all have always been ones that have been real for me since day one. Rest in Heaven and see you soon.

I also want to dedicate this book to all of my loving family and friends that have been supportive to me as I have faced and overcame this challenge. May God bless you and be with you always.

Last but not least I want to dedicate this book to all stroke survivors and those who have overcome challenges that may have seemed too tough to overcome, but stand today as living witnesses that with God all things are possible.

Acknowledgments

I would like to recognize my Uncle Sam Beattie who helped raise me and taught me about being a man. At an early age, he stepped up and not told me about just life but living in its fullness.

I would like to recognize my Father and Mother, Tim Beattie Sr and Deborah Conerly who have always been there for me mentally, physically, spiritually as a guide of light and a mold of inspiration.

I want to recognize my Auntie Sharon Davis who has been extremely helpful and loving through this tough and adverse time.

I like to shout out the therapy team at Saint Francis Park, and to my favorite trainers Leslie and Kim for all their hard work and dedication. You guys gave not only your passion, but your hearts into helping me get back to normal functions daily.

A special shout out to my ex-wife Tabatha Morris-Beattie for all that you have done showing that God is truly a God of love. Your admiration daily has allowed me to become strengthen mentally, physically, and spiritually. I truly thank you and love you for all that you have done throughout this time. I can't thank you enough for what you did daily and especially throughout my transition back home.

Last but not least, I would like to Thank my loving kids Trey, Triston, and Autumn. Seeing you all daily has truly motivated me to get back to the point, where Our lives can continue in love, Joy, and peace. Seeing you all grow these last few months has been truly a blessing. I pray that my experience has been alive in you and empowered you to be better and stronger in Christ as you grow older in life.

I love you always,

Dad

Table of Contents

Chapter 1: The Beginning

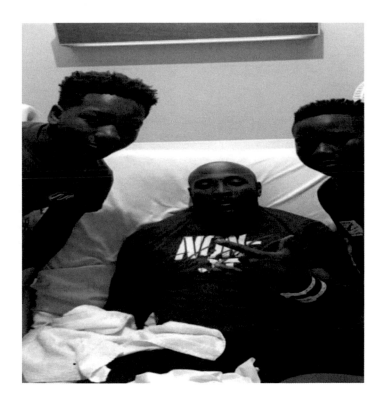

May 30, 1979, I was born in the small city of Shreveport located in Louisiana. My dad was in the Air Force and mom was a woman who was filled with so much love, charisma, talent, and service. As a baby, I had no idea that my life would take a change so fast, but neither did my parents. Make a commitment at such a young age, but chasing love usually leads us to face life's ups and downs, but that's another story. My parents eventually divorced due to all the things you could imagine that takes place in a broken relationship.

I ended up going to Memphis Tn., to live with my Dad and my grandmother, but living with my Dad ended up with just living with my grandmother and my uncle who eventually raised me. My Dad chose the streets, drugs, partying, and anything that wasn't a part of being a father and raising his kids.

My Dad eventually found his home away from home at Fort Pillow Correction Center for almost 8- years. So, growing up as a young teen in the hood and when I say the hood, I mean it was the hood, every kid in Hyde Park had to face tough and hard situations daily. The opposition of drugs, gangs, and poverty was already a lot to deal with daily along with not having your mother or father to teach you and lead you with handling the ins and outs of life each day was rough.

For example, In the 4th grade, I was kicked out of school for bringing a knife to school, as an 11th grader, I was kicked out of school for being falsely accused of 8 counts of aggravated assault and 8 counts of aggravated rape that eventually was dropped because the kids stepped up and admitted the principal told them to make the accusation (racism at its best).

Even in college, I was kicked out of school for being in a fight in our football locker room. I know you probably saying wow and that I've been through a lot. Well, I have and that's not half of it, but what I do want you to know is that I was built for adversity. I was created to overcome situations that the average person couldn't defeat. You have to know who you are and your purpose in life. When God makes it clear to you that these situations are not to tear you down, but to build you up, so that he can make you better. So that you can win when the major test is presented— all you can do is just persevere.

So, don't let that pressure cause you to explode and lose everything that God has for you. Learn from the weights that might be heavy on you and take those weights and lift them up off of you and become stronger. One situation or one rep at a time, get better, get stronger, and overcome. You have to know how special and how important you are. Those who will be great will always face more obstacles than those who are average. From my conception into this world, my life was predestined and designed for greatness. Take a moment and think about yourself right now...................see what I'm saying, your life was designed for greatness too.

Today, I encourage you to fight-- I encourage you to overcome, I encourage you to give when giving seems as if you've given all you have. You have to know that your life may sometimes seem like you are in the fight of your life, but the fight of your life may just be the fight that prepares you for the journey that God is about to carry you through for the rest of your life.

As you read this book about the trials and tribulations of my life, I hope that it motivates you and draws you closer to Christ, allowing you to build your faith, and enhance your relationship with

Christ through your actions at home, at work, at church, in the community or where ever you may be daily. My story is not built for tears of sadness but tears of hope. I want to leave you with one fact as you journey ahead through this book packed with motivation. When I woke up in the hospital and saw all these people in my room surrounding me, I said to myself God Why Me, he said I needed to use you so others can draw closer to me. Immediately I knew where things were headed.

As you read the book, I will elaborate later on this more and help you understand how we got to September 1st.

Chapter 2: Life As A Kid

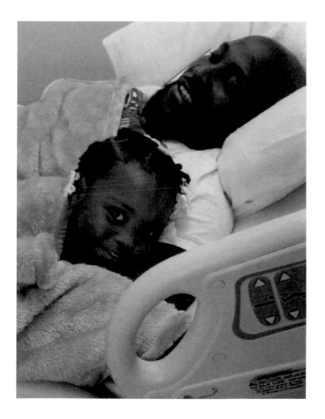

As a kid growing up in Hyde Park it seemed like the most enjoyable place to be daily was playing

chase through the neighborhood, jacks, hopscotch, jump rope, hide-go-&-seek, put back, pick up and run, or building club houses with Uncle Clyde's junk, climbing trees, shooting hoops, and so much more. My neighborhood was one like no other— but as a kid, I also had to learn how to survive daily. I grew up next door to a crack house, saw drugs sold right before my eyes, heard or saw shootings as if it was the norm. And dealt with the everyday shenanigans from local gang members. This was life for me, the good, the bad, the pretty, and the ugly but it was my neighborhood, Hyde Park. A neighborhood that had your back no matter right or wrong— it was a family outside of the family.

I grew up on Lyon street, across from the Turners, down the street from the Jenkins. These were my two hangout spots daily. Either I was down the street with Meaty or across the street with Kevin and Terry. Growing up, I and Meaty were best friends, we did everything together. Almost, like what you see in the movies. I mean we would build clubhouses, steal and build bikes, go in the corner store with 54 cents and share the chips and drink, fight each other and be back hanging within 10- minutes, but we were like brothers, we weren't gonna let nobody bother us, didn't matter who you were. Now, Kevin and Terry were brothers and younger than me. I would play football, basketball, and just sit on the porch with them and talk about the girls in the neighborhood.

As we all grew older, we all went down separate paths of life. My path led me towards playing football— I remember one day at Shannon Elementary in the cafeteria some of my friends asked me to come to play football for the Evergreen Chiefs. Now, the closet thing I had been to playing football was 2 on 2 in the street or pick up and run, and playing in the street was more about being able to catch and score. So, my dad ended up taking me to Gooch park and my expedition for my life began.

So, we made it to Gooch park and all the jitterbugs and nervousness was there with me.

It started with us running two laps to begin practice. I ran those 2- laps so fast trying to impress the coach because I thought we were all competing for 1st place. I wish somebody would've told me cause after we finished, I found out that it were only warm-up laps— but because I had this drive and competitive edge in me, the coach saw something in me. He asked me after we finished running "What position you play," and my answer was wide-receiver, but only because I loved Jerry Rice and didn't realize my height played a factor in what position I would play. But I was only a kid and just loved competing and winning, but the coach said no, you a running back.

I was so fast my teammates started calling me Lil fie feet, in other words, "Fire feet" because I was that fast.

For me, Football was becoming all I wanted to do. I started being one of the first to get to practice and one of the last to leave. I loved it so much that sometimes I would walk to the Coach house just to be on time or to ride with him to pick up other players. Little did I know that my skills as a leader were growing within me and before I knew it the guys were depending on me to lead them to a Championship.

As a kid, I can remember being about 9 years old and my cousin Du'juan was playing football for Cypress Jr High, while I played for the Chiefs— each week, they would lose a game and we would lose a game and his question to me was always "Are yall gonna regroup this week," and I'd always ask him the same in return. Him asking me that made me know that he had faith in me leading my team and that he knew that I had what it takes to be a game-changer at such a young age— it's amazing what others can see in us before we can see it in ourselves. For him, it was his way of challenging me and instilling in me the mold for being a leader.

He could see my passion, desire, and commitment from our long talks daily after practice. So, I believe he knew he had to push me to step up and stop talking about it and to be about it.

Nevertheless, it happened! It was Saturday and we were playing the redskins. It was a hot day, I had my favorite 3- striped socks on and brand new pro-wing cleats. I was just feeling like today is the day. We hit the field all hype, beating our pads on one accord— the game started off with both teams battling going back and forth, but with no score. So now, it's the 4th quarter with less than 2-minutes on the clock. Our QB gets hurt and Coach John Lucky moves me to QB and calls 18 roll which is a QB Keep. I walked to the line, went through my cadence, Down, Set, and fire. The ball is snapped and there I go around the edge untouched for a 50- yard touchdown. I'm in the end zone for my first touchdown ever, the team is excited and we're celebrating to only find out that it's coming back due to a holding penalty. I mean, it was one of the best feelings ever. But we have to huddle up and score again. Everybody is motivated that we can do it, but frustrated at the same time.

The time is running down and Coach Lucky calls time out. Our QB is back in the game and the Coach says we're running 28- reverse to Tj, I'm extra amped up because I wanted to score and win the ball game. We're in the huddle and everyone is like get in the end zone. To have everyone depending on me was easy and just an amazing feeling. So, here we go again, we come out the huddle and line up. I line up to the left at tight end but off the ball— the ball is snapped and we fake the toss to the left, but hand me the ball going back right.

Everything develops so fast before the defense realized that I had the ball I was halfway to the end zone. All I could hear was the commentator over the PA system saying Touchdown. Our entire team rushed the field as the clock ran out and there you have it. Our first win, we had finally regrouped and won a ball game. I couldn't wait to go home and tell my cousin, but that day was the beginning of a tradition for us all. We didn't end up winning the championship that year, but I was named an MVP.

We never know how some traits like being a leader will be instilled in us. I never knew that day would forever be one that I would be seen as a leader. My life was no longer the same from that day. I knew that I was born to be a winner, motivator, leader, and inspiration to those around me. But that was only the beginning of what God had planned for my life— I didn't realize it then that God was preparing me then for who I am now.

We have to understand that preparation is key. In order for us to carry out the mission that God has for our lives, we shall and we must be prepared. The United States armed forces don't just wake up and go to war. The Chicago Bulls didn't win 6- NBA rings just because they had Michael Jordan. President Obama didn't become the First Black President and doing it with greatness with luck. These things happened because they were prepared and were willing to go through the process of preparation. Being prepared means that you go through training mentally, physically, and spiritually. Mentally your mind has to be conditioned, physically your body is taught endurance, and Spiritually you learn and **gain wisdom about the human condition throughout life.**

Chapter 3: It Happened

It was a great sunny Sunday afternoon when I and the kids decided to spend our day at the fair. We woke up that morning excited about spending time together eating corn dogs, funnel cakes, and riding rides just like any other family had expected that day.

So, after getting dressed and cleaning up— we headed off to the fair. We just knew we were going to have a great day full of fun and activities. With our first stop being the fair and I second stop at my auntie's house for our annual day of family- fun, our day was set.

So, eventually, we made it to the fair in order to get our corn dogs, wristbands, and ice cream that we had talked about all night before reaching the fair the following day. We quickly headed to the fun with my son Trey starting the day off by playing with the snake that one of the workers had on display. It was funny and crazy to see my son step out on a limb and do something so silly. It reminded me when he was only five years old and I took him out to the Circus. On that day at the circus, I took him down to take a picture of petting a snake to only see him scream and yell to get away from the snake. It was such a funny scene that we actually caught it as the photographer snapped away the picture.

As time went by, the kids ran around, played games, and ate lots of food as they enjoyed every moment possible at the fair. We were having so much fun that I almost forget about going to my aunties house for our family get together until I got the call from my auntie Sharon was asking where are you? And are you still coming? Of course, I was coming, one to eat the good food, two to play some spades, and three to see my Uncle Sammy pull off some of his funny antics that had everyone full of laughs from the last family get together. So we loaded up and headed to my Aunt Sharon's house So finally arrived and what we found was a house full of family, food, and fellowship.

We get to the house and The first thing I do is lay my daughter down to take a nap. With all the fun at the fair, she has quickly nodded off to sleep. Next, I take my normal stroll through the house meeting and greeting, laughing and joking. We have only been there about 10- minutes and I was talking to my Aunt Debbie about the kids, work, and just life. As we were talking, I was standing and became a little dizzy— I'm sure she didn't recognize as we were talking so I took a seat and continued to talk to her.

As we talked, I just didn't feel right so, I left out the room to just regroup alone. I figured that since we had been in the heat that I just needed to gather myself for a minute and that I would be okay. Well, after a minute of sitting alone, I had my son get my Uncle Sammy because I could feel myself getting worse. So, my uncle comes in and asked what's wrong? As I began to go through the process, my uncle being my uncle ask me "Did you have some of that Funny Juice" and immediately we both start laughing because he's referring to alcohol.

So, we ended up calling 9-1-1, at this point, things for me were declining. Within moments, I noticed that both my arms were completely dead. I had no function within my arms. My cousin Monique who is a nurse was assessing me and was reassuring me that I wasn't showing any signs of a stroke, but she didn't understand why my arms were without any function.

As she stated this, it kind of put me in a place of calmness, but at the same time, I was scared because I didn't know what was going on and then, to look around and see the faces of my loved ones in shock, despair, confusion, and fear didn't help me during my current situation— it seemed as if everyone was afraid. You would think that with a praying grandmother that our resemblance of Faith would've been demonstrated beyond measure, but what was shown was the humanistic behaviors that we all display known as love. I knew that at this point that they all were praying in the spirit, and that's what we call Beattie Strong.

But eventually, the ambulance arrived and assessed me on the spot. I remember the ambulance saying you look great, but I'm not sure why your arms are numb so, let's get you to the ambulance so we can take you to the hospital and see what's wrong. My stress level immediately went from 10 to 0 hearing the ambulance say that. At this point, mentally I was like I will be okay once I get to the hospital. So as I attempted to get up I noticed that both my legs had gone dead as well, which took me to a level of freight that I had never experienced before.

My uncles and cousins gathered around me and began to lift me in order to carry me to the ambulance. As I was being carried out, I could only think about my kids as I exited the door. By the time we made it to the ambulance, I was completely out of it. We eventually made it to the hospital and what seemed like only a few minutes had been hours of tests and prayers, and then, lights out. I went into a coma for 6- days.

Not knowing what was really going to come of this situation, I could only imagine the thoughts that ran through the minds of my loved ones. My parents, uncles, aunties, cousins, my kids, and even my friends. With me laying in a state of unconsciousness, a place where I had no control of my physical state, a place in which the mind is inaccessible to the conscious mind. A place where hope activates the faith, a place where no one but the Father, our Lord and Savior Jesus Christ could go and restore and heal beyond measure— while everyone was trying to make sense of things, God was working and doing exactly what he does.

So, the doctors had informed everyone that I had suffered from an Aneurysm that caused my stroke. Now, an Aneurysm often occurs in the aorta, brain, back of the knee, intestine, or spleen. A ruptured aneurysm can result in internal bleeding, stroke, and can sometimes be fatal. The concern for an aneurysm is that they are deadly. About 10% of patients with a ruptured aneurysm die before receiving medical care, If untreated, another 50% will die within a month. So, now you understand how serious it was and what could've been, but never happened due to God's grace and Mercy.

So, the doctor had informed my family that I had an aneurysm or brain bleed and that were a few things they should know. First, that it was a must that they operate in order to save my life, next that if everything went well that it would be about 2- years before I would walk or talk again. Now, this had to be the most horrific news that anyone could hear. One, it was labor day and we were supposed to be enjoying each other with love and fellowship and two, how could this be happening,. I could only imagine that it must've felt so heartbreaking and the emotions of everyone was all over the place.

The next few days for everyone had to be tough, but at the same time, I truly believe that the prayer warriors of my family and friends had not just begun, but had increased not in numbers but in faith. As the time came near, it was time for me to prepare for surgery, in other words, time for God to show his power. As the nurses prepared me and as the doctors went through their normal assessments, God reigned and did what he has always done numerous times before me. Isaiah 53:5 reminds us that by "His" stripes we are healed. In that time as the doctors scanned the machines and so on, they noticed that there were no signs of any aneurysm in my brain. They told my family that is was like it never happened and that the only thing to do now was to monitor me for progress over the next few days.

The Power of God is and has always been evident in my life. God had saved my life to only remind me that I have a purpose and that he wasn't done with using me just yet. We have to realize the power that is within us and the magnitude that God has planned to use in us in order to bring others to Christ.

In the book of Job, Satan knew that Job was faithful and committed to God. Satan figured that if he only had the chance that he would be able to break Job down and get him to the point where he would curse God and give up. One thing you must never forget is that God will never leave you nor forsake you. You must never forget that you are a child of God, you must never forget that the weapons of the enemy may form and try to break you down in every angle but know that they will not prosper.

 I say this to say that even when Satan tried to attack my mind, my body, and my soul, God had me covered. That God is our refuge and strength, that even when we walk through the valley of the shadows of death that he will be with us. A long time ago I figured it out, that everything I stood on would eventually come down to my faith. Being in ministry I realized that most of my teachings dealt with faith. Mainly because I was a faith walker. I've always said that if you don't have faith what do you have.

I realize now that the one thing that you truly believe in will be the one thing you will eventually be tested with. For me, it was my faith. As men and women of God, we teach others of the word of God daily, and eventually, the Word draws you to a specific that caters to you and that will become how you live in the world. Know that word is real because eventually God's test will be right before your eyes, STAND ON IT and watch God move miraculously in your life.

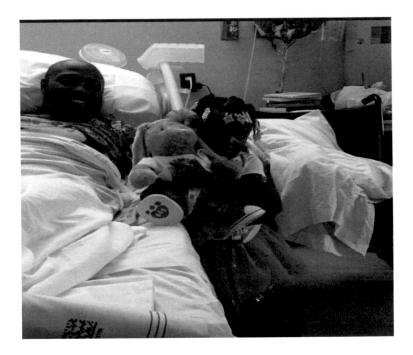

In every sport, there is a half-time that takes place. This half time is usually a time were the players and coaches have time to reassess themselves and the team so that they can either bounce back or continue to move forward. For me, this was an opportunity for me to bounce back and move forward in my life— to bounce back means to return quickly to a normal condition after a difficult situation or event. Here, I am waking up without any knowledge of what I've actually been through, what is actually taking place, or what lies before me in the days to come. As I open my eyes and began to scan the room, I can vaguely see the people around me due to the rest that my body needs. It's more of the sounds of voices that lead me in the direction of loved ones whether family or friends with words of encouragement and laughs in the background as I go in and out, sleeping and waking.

After a few days of sleeping and waking, but mostly sleeping, my body was starting to restore and regain strength. I can remember the day and the first sign of me getting stronger. The nurse woke me up to let me know they were about to remove the feeding tube from my throat. I guess the tube had been in my throat so long that I didn't even notice it being there with me sleeping so much. This was one of the worst things ever, the pulling and tugging felt like they were trying to kill me.

I promise that tube was so far down my throat, I almost vomited as they removed it from my throat. It was so bad that they literally had to hold me down in order to finish removing it. Once they finished, I was trying to get my breathing together, I was coughing and spitting— it was just a horrible experience that took me a few minutes to recover from.

After the nurses left that was when I realized that my stroke was a very serious situation. I was laying in the bed quietly looking around at my family and I remember reaching my arm out trying to get the attention of my cousin Nick. I was attempting to tell him that I was going to be alright and that I appreciated them all, but as I spoke he kept responding as if he couldn't understand me. I then noticed that because he couldn't understand me that he wanted to console me by just saying everything would be alright and that I should just get some rest. It was at that split second that I realized that what I was saying was like a mumbling of words to him. My mind began to ramble with so many things within that moment. First, I became so frustrated out of fear that I would never be able to speak again and communicate with others.

Secondly, I thought about my friend Tionne when he had his stroke. I thought and said that the nurses were always right. That he could hear everything we were saying. I could hear clearly what everyone around me was saying, it was just me that they couldn't understand. It all made sense to me now, Tionne would always just smile when we talked about football or the Cowboys.

Mentally, with all this racing through my brain, I was breaking and about to explode but immediately the fight in me kicked in and I closed my eyes and prayed to God. Within that moment I thanked God for all he had done for me. All he had taken me through, and what he was about to do with me at that very moment. It was then that it hit me. God needed to use me to reach those who were connected to me including, family, friends, co-workers, social media etc. Remember before chapter 1 told you I asked God Why Me, he said I needed to use you so others can draw closer to me. Well, it was clear what the mission was at this point and what is really the reason I have been able to push harder every day.

When you realize you have a divine purpose mandated by God to help establish the Kingdom of God then it makes the journey a lot more possible. Just thinking back, I had previously re-established my church home at New Bethel Missionary Baptist Church under the leadership of Pastor Mathis where I was on fire, preaching, teaching, and just began working with the men's ministry.

I was seeing the works of my labor manifest before my own eyes. But nearly did I know it, God was planning greater than I could imagine. But in order for this task to take place I would have to endure what would seem endless for others but fearless for me.

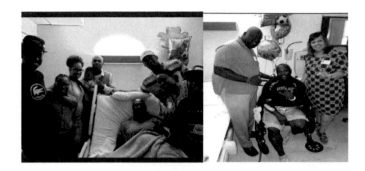

It's been a few days and I've been transferred to where my therapy will be taking place. For me, I've got this picture in my head that I'm going to go in therapy hit the weights and do all these exercises and be back to normal in no time. But what I didn't realize was that my body had change. That the last twenty plus years of beasting in the gym was gone, though, the drive and motivation I possessed was still there, just not the strength.

When we think about recovery, we think of the ability to return, reclaim, retrieve, or regain something to a normal state of health, mind, or strength. Recovery for me was all of this when it comes to my physical, mental, and spiritual state of being.

It wasn't that I didn't have fortitude mentally, physically, or spiritually. It was just accepting that my ship had been wrecked. That it was going to take a real master plan to fix what had happened. Let me help you understand what I mean. I was a kid who was built for adversity, challenges, obstacles or whatever you wanted to throw in front of me. I lived for it daily. If it was something you said I couldn't do, then you better know I was ready to take it head-on. I grew up in an era that it was a blessing just to see your 18th birthday or graduate high school, and I did that with ease while growing up in the heart of North Memphis. I faced adversity as it was nothing, I grew up in a home where my grandmother raised me without any financial support from my parents. I went to college and played football as a walk-on freshman and ended up earning a full scholarship within 2- weeks of being in summer camp, I later graduated college with honors maintaining a 3.3 GPA. See some people dream about overcoming circumstances and situations but it's something I've been doing my entire life.

So, for me to be here laying in this bed with limited mobility physically and a deficiency in my speech, for some it would seem impossible to recover, but for me and how I was raised, nothing was impossible for God. Knowing I was a man of God, a man of faith. I believed and knew that this was a journey that I had to travel, a mountain I could climb, curves that would be bumpy, but something I knew I could handle.

When I was a kid and things would get tough for me, I'd sit down and talk with my grandmother. She was a very spiritual woman and every time those conversations would end she would always remind me that the race isn't given to the swift nor to the strongest but to the one who endures to the end. My grandmother planted a seed in me with this scripture that grew into a foundation for my life. This became a part of how I lived no matter if it was in sports, jobs, relationships, etc. As

I prepared to go on with my therapy I had to remember that this wasn't about how strong I was, but it was about me finishing and enduring no matter what I faced.

So, I remember getting up that first-day eating breakfast, taking my meds, having my morning devotion, and sitting patiently waiting to go to therapy. I remember it like it was yesterday. My door swings open and this black lady comes in with all this energy, smiling, loud and very enthused saying good morning Tim my name is Leslie I will be working with you, are you ready to go. I'm kind of dry with her responding yes. I mean this lady was a real firecracker. She is rolling me down the hall asking me where I'm from, how old are you, as so on and in my head, I'm like I don't want to talk, I just want to do my therapy— it was funny because not only was I ready to work, she was ready to work. I mean I had this tough guy attitude like I got this let me just show you but in reality, I learned that day that if I wanted to get better that I was going to have to swallow my pride and be willing to trust her each day. That was very hard for me at first because my entire life I've had to do thing s myself. If I wanted something I had to get it. Everybody from family, friends, and relationships that I ever put my trust in had let me down. Now I have to completely trust her with being able to walk again.

Daily it was a battle mentally and physically. I mean she would come in smiling each morning and would literally work me to death. It was like my freshman year of college football. You never got to the point that you got used to the workouts because she would push you more and more each day. The workouts were so crucial that I hated walking. I know you probably saying how could you hate walking if you wanted to walk again. Well, it was more like a love and hate relationship. Meaning I loved making the progress daily and hearing Leslie say you think you got one more in you today or I need you to walk 30ft, 60ft, 90ft, so we just gonna walk today. That was the motivation for her to push me and not just to settle but to push me to raise the bar each day. On the opposite side of that, it was tough learning how to walk all over. Something I had learned as a baby I had to re-learn at 40 years old. That meant that there was a lot of bad behaviors or mechanics that needed fixing. So as I took steps and had to remember to shift my weight, tighten my quad muscles to activate them was a lot. My mind and body were both processing things at two different times on different scales.

After a few weeks of physical therapy and I am coming out of my shell, they ended up changing schedule and switching me to a new physical therapist and scheduled me for occupational therapy. I honestly didn't like it at all because I felt like I was making so much progress. So, immediately I went back into my shell. I had just gotten to the point where I was trusting Leslie and from my observation, I felt like she was the best to work with me so I could get back to walking. I mean I had set goals and expectations and now what am I going to do, but I had to realize that being in my feelings was only going to set me back.

So, I started my first week with my new therapist and I wasn't happy at all. Every day it seemed as if I was working with someone different and every day seemed like day one. I say this because the therapist wasn't sure of what I could or couldn't do so it was like an evaluation each day— I had people depending on me, but here I am going backwards.

At least I thought I was, I never fully understood the mode of recovery until I went through it myself. I'm reminded that even in the early days that soldiers would leave home and go to fight battles that would last days and sometimes months. Even in the midst of the battle the soldiers didn't retreat but would fall back just to recover. For them, recovery meant to rest or even reevaluate the strategy to make sure they were taking the right steps to be successful. In this very moment, I realized that God knew that I had been pounding day after day 6- days a week and that I needed a few days of rest and recovery. A few days for me to self-examine and reevaluate the course that God had carried me thus far. Sometimes we get a little anxious and want to interject ourselves in the plan. We have to remember that Gods ways are not our ways neither are Gods thoughts our thoughts. That's why his word tells us to trust in him and not to lean to our own understanding but in all our ways to acknowledge him and he will direct our paths.

Then it happens, I get a bright morning and here comes in a lady with the country daisy duke accent, Good Morning I'm Kim I'm going to be your new occupational therapist. For me I'm in the here we go again mode but had no idea how my progress was about to elevate to the next level. I mean Kim and Leslie were like the dynamic duo just working in two different specialties. But Kim had a gift that was like no other. Kim not only had the skills and knowledge for an occupational therapist, but she had the skills and knowledge to be a physical therapist as well. I had been positioned to get the best of both worlds.

Although, she wasn't my physical therapist, she gave me pointers of things I could do in my room while sitting around daily. When she had extra time, she would come to get me and work with me. I felt like I was winning and that I was on top of the world, but before I give you all the oweees and aweess, let me back up and let you know how we got to this point. I remember I had got up and completed my normal routine as I would always do and had just prayed to God that I wasn't going to allow Satan any room to make me lose focus that day.

Well, I was struggling that morning, had just finished showering and couldn't get my clothes on, socks, or shoes, hand, arm, leg, and foot were all having one of those days. Kim was trying to help me and give me suggestions but I was trying to be independent and do it my way and that just wasn't working. Not only was my body tripping but I wasn't in the mood physically. The lady I was currently dating had left me as well. So, I was all over the place. I literally went off on Kim. I felt so horrible because I had let all my frustrations out on her rather than handling it better. So as she was taking me to therapy I stopped and just prayed. The devil was doing exactly what I said I didn't want to happen and I refused to let it go on any further. I apologized and it was like a sudden change in the atmosphere— that was the day that changed everything.

I went from being a pain in the butt to one of the hardest working clients that she ever had. One thing that made Leslie and Kim so good is they build relationships with their clients. They find out who they are, to know how exactly how to meet the needs of the client. I was an ex-football player so they knew how to push me and how to motivate me. Therapy with Kim was amazing. At times I felt like I was her guinea pig when it came to workouts. You guys who are trainers know that as a trainer you are always looking for that one person who you can try out your more advanced workouts on just to see how well they work. Well, I was that person! I mean these workouts were extreme but I also knew that they were pushing me beyond my limit in a good way because she was always saying we gone do this or that today but I don't know how much you gonna be able to do. In my head, I would laugh because I knew this was her way of trying to push me and I believe she knew that was sparking that fire of competition that was molded deep down inside of me.

Chapter 6: Progress With Purpose

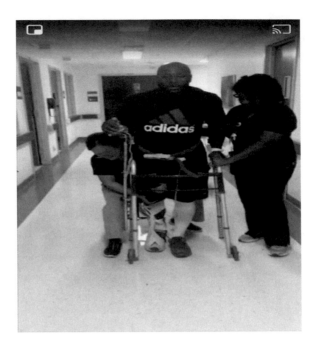

As time went on I progressed more and more and each day I began to take steps that I had been expecting since day 1. I finally was taking steps towards walking, something I hadn't done since before my stroke.

It's amazing how we as humans have the ability daily to walk, run, jump and so much more, but take it for granted each day when it can be gone within the split of a second. Never did I imagine in my worst dream that my ability to walk would be gone from me. But here I was in therapy taking steps like a baby, not trusting my legs due to the weakness and spasticity in my body. Every step was a win and a moment of hope that one day I would be back to walking as I had before.

For me, it was about making progress with purpose. I knew that this stroke could break me mentally, physically, and spiritually if I don't push daily. I wanted my life back and there wasn't going to be anything that would stop me. I was so focused that I didn't just operate on faith alone. My belief in God never wavered but my confidence in myself was where I was struggling. I know you are probably saying how could that be. Well, there were somethings I had to overcome in order for me to get back to the Beattie you all once fell in love with.

So, one of the first struggles was being weak physically. All my life I had built this persona of being a gym rat lifting weights and getting extra buff and now I couldn't lift a 5-pounds dumbbell. This definitely brought my confidence down to an all-time low. This meant I couldn't protect myself or my kids if I was ever put in that situation. Being strong physically was part of who I had become. Body By Beattie, Touchdown TJ, and Beattie Boy was all known as this strong fit guy. As a kid to a man being in the gym was one area of how I had built my confidence. Everybody has that one thing that helps distinguish themselves from others and this was it for me.

Next, I couldn't take care of myself when it came to my hygiene or even using the bathroom without help— during my early phases of being in the hospital this part of recovery was one that made me feel less than a man. To have female nurses to come in a shower me, change my clothes, and even having to wipe my butt after taking a dump was definitely a horrible feeling. Even in this process I was dating a female who I thought was decent and caring who one day just up and broke up with me after 5 months of dating. At that point, my confidence was shot and I was just feeling like crap.

But if you know anything about me nothing ever keeps me down. You know what they say, what don't kill you will make you stronger. And it did, that next morning I was beginning my day with the focus to become more independent for myself so that when I left I could take care of me and not depend on anyone. I remember that day like it was yesterday. I knew that breakfast would be coming around 8:00 so I woke up at 6 am, washed up, brushed my teeth, changed my clothes, and did my morning devotion. Yes, I did all this after becoming so dependent on nurses and my ex-girlfriend. When my nurse came in to do all those things she was shocked. One thing we can't ever forget is that the mind is a very powerful thing. Once you set your mind on anything, you can accomplish it. I was so focused on making progress with the purpose that my nurses started to believe and know that I was going to do great. What I want and need for you to understand is that your progress needs to have a purpose. When you set and understand your purpose, you will create a vision for where you are going, and seeing is believing. Because I had these steps in the order that I could move forward without any distractions.

I can remember being in therapy and confined to my hospital room daily– it had been almost a month and the closet thing I had seen to being outside was looking out my bedroom window. I wanted to go outside so bad and feel the breeze and the sunlight hit my skin. You know, that feeling of life as if I was in Miami on the beach. So, one day I told my nurse that I wanted to go outside because I've been in here locked up. She was excited and had cut my work out a little short so that I could go outside towards the end. She went and threw on her shades and we left. We jumped on the elevator and headed out. I had no idea what to expect, I just wanted to go outside. Here I am wheeling myself off the elevator to see so many people. It was like being downtown on Beale Street on a Saturday night. I was so used to being in my room all day that I forgot what it was like to be in a normal setting.

So, I began to maneuver through the crowd looking in every direction just amused with the people and interactions taking place that I totally forgot about going outside. We eventually made it to the door and I began to glow with the joy of going outside and it kind of felt like a relief to just leave that building and get out of that atmosphere. As we exited the door I had no idea what I was about to experience and boom it hits me. The sun is bright and overwhelming but so overwhelming I couldn't bear the sight at being in the light. One of the effects of my stroke caused the sunlight to become very sensitive to my eyes. I felt like I had been blinded and that my vision was completely gone.

I had awaited this moment for so long and to get outside and have such a horrible experience was very disheartening. The light was so bad that my nurse had to rush me back inside. I had to cover my eyes and even once I returned inside I still couldn't open my eyes to endure the light until moment's right before making back to my room. I learned that no matter what we want or how bad we want something it's important that we are prepared for the situation. Although my nurse wasn't suffering from any medical conditions she was prepared for the situation. Her taking the time just to grab her shades prepared her for the moment. Life is filled with obstacles that lead to opportunities for us to prepare for the many journeys of life. What matters most is how we prepare mentally, physically, and spiritually. If you aren't prepared, then it will be easy for you to be blinded and keep you from seeing the road that lies ahead of you. Always remember that in order to make progress that requires purpose and together that makes your vision more clear so that you can accomplish your journey that lies ahead.

Chapter 7 The Race Isn't Finished

Over the past 8 months, a lot has happened since being discharged from the hospital. I went from

being in a wheelchair to walking with a cane, to now walking with a boot to now taking steps

without any assistance. Although, I'm not at 100 per cent in walking and complete mobility in my hand it has been a journey that I will continue to stay on pace until I complete the race. As I steady the course, I'm always reminded of my grandmother who constantly reminded me that the race isn't given to the swift nor to the strongest, but to the one who endures till the end. When I took on this course I knew it would be ups and downs, bumps and curves, and so much more. But I knew that God had me the entire time and if I just trusted him I would make it without a shadow of a doubt. In my life, I've always been very big on having faith. No matter what I always caught myself teaching and preaching about having faith or If it was a friend going through something or a family member feeling like giving up my first thing was always you must have faith and this is a time to stand on your faith.

One thing that life has taught me is that whatever you believe in when it comes to the word of God, it will eventually be that one thing that will be right before you. And when it's before you how will you respond. Will you be as Peter and deny what you have followed and believed in. Or will you be like Job and continue to believe in God. Faith is believing with your entire heart that no matter the situation you want give up on God.

I've had the opportunity to see the power of God operate in my life like never before. I want to share with you a few verses that I prayed daily for my healing. I don't know what you are going through, have been through, or what may be ahead but I believe these verses will help you to endure through it all.

(Matthew 7:7,8) Ask and it will be given to you; seek and you will find; knock and the door will be opened to you. [8] For everyone who asks receives; the one who seeks finds; and to the one who knocks, the door will be opened.

(Matthew 21:22) If you believe, you will receive whatever you ask for in prayer.

(Mark 11:24) Therefore I tell you, whatever you ask for in prayer, believe that you have received it, and it will be yours."

(Proverbs 15:29) The LORD is far from the wicked, but he hears the prayer of the righteous.

(Jeremiah 33:3) Call to me and I will answer you and tell you great and unsearchable things you do not know.'

(Matthew 6:6) But when you pray, go into your room, close the door and pray to your unseen Father. Then, your Father, who sees what is done in secret, will reward you.

(1 John 3:22), and receive from him anything we ask, because we keep his commands and do what pleases him.

These scriptures are promises from God. It was my duty daily to pray to God of the things he promised me. As I prayed I believed and I saw God begin to heal me and restore the things in which I had lost. I had enough hope that when I prayed I activated my faith. You may one day be functioning as normal and tomorrow the doctors could diagnose you with cancer, kidney failure, or even a bad heart. My question for you is where is your faith? God needs to know that you believe. He doesn't need you to have a wavering faith but one that trusts him. And it's not about how much you believe because his word says you can have faith the size of a mustard seed. So know that the race isn't finished until you have run the race that God wants you to complete. Each of us has been placed in the world for specific missions. So run till you can't run anymore, and when you can't run anymore crawl.

Today I'm about 77-80% healthy within 8 months of having my aneurysm. And my race isn't finished. I thank God for using me to be a tool to bring those who don't know Christ to Christ, and to rekindle relationships with Christ. It's truly an honor to share my testimony with others to encourage, equip, and empower others as they take on their journey of faith. I love you all but my love will one day end. But always remember that the Love of God will last forever.

Made in the USA
Middletown, DE
07 July 2020

12178679R00024